A Christmas Pit

A Peter "Pit" Geller Caper

A CHRISTMAS PIT

JOHN GREGORY BETANCOURT

A Christmas Pit

Published by Wildside Press

Visit us online at wildsidepress.com

A CHRISTMAS PIT

When my doorbell rang, the sound jolted through me like an electric shock. I accidentally sloshed Jack Daniel's across my lap and began cursing all unexpected visitors.

Carefully, so I wouldn't spill another drop, I set the bottle on my night table, grabbed my walking stick, and swung my ruined legs over the side of the bed. Standing usually hurt, but I'd already drunk enough to feel a comfortable numbness instead.

The doorbell rang a second time, an annoying *brzzz* that set my teeth on edge.

"Stop that racket! I'm coming!" I yelled. I shrugged a robe over my underwear, knotting the belt halfheartedly, and limped out into my rather Spartan family room.

By the time I turned the deadbolt and yanked open the front door, I half expected to find the hallway deserted. The brats upstairs enjoyed playing jokes like that — "bait the cripple," I called it.

Tonight, however, I found a soggy young man in an Atlanta Braves baseball cap and a cheap brown coat. Water pooled around him and the duffel bag he'd set down. Rain — that explained why my legs had been aching worse than usual.

"What do you want?" I demanded. "Don't you know what time it is?"

Involuntarily, he covered his mouth and nose and took a half step back. I had to reek like a distillery.

"Uh...six o'clock?" he said. His voice had a slight southern twang.

"Oh." Only six o'clock? My sense of time was shot; I would have sworn it was past midnight. "I thought it was later than that. It gets dark early now."

"Are you...Peter Geller?" he asked hesitantly.

"Yes. You're here to see *me*?"

"Sir... David Hunt sent me."

I had gone to college with Davy. We had been in the same fraternity. Since Davy came from old money, he got in because his family had always belonged. I got in because I was smart: all the jocks and rich kids needed help to keep up their GPAs. Sometimes I had resented it, being used, but it got me into all the parties, and I still graduated at the top of our class.

My life had been a downward spiral after college. I had landed a plum job at an investment bank, but overwork and my always-racing mind led to a nervous breakdown. Six months later, a taxi ran me over and left me permanently crippled. I lost touch with everyone I'd ever known and began trying to drink myself to death, until Davy called me out of the blue to help him out when he was being blackmailed. That had been five months ago. We'd had dinner and drinks a dozen times since then, rekindling our old friendship. In fact, earlier this afternoon I had been wondering what to give Davy for Christmas. He already had everything money could buy.

"Are you some sort of social worker?" I asked warily.

"No, sir! I'm Bob Charles." At my puzzled look, he added, "Cree's brother."

"Got any I.D.?"

"Uh...sure." He dug around his coat's inside pocket. "Driver's license? Passport?"

"Either."

He handed me a military passport. Marine Corps issue, and the name under his picture read "PFC Robert E. Charles."

I nodded, my mental wheels starting to turn. Cree was the actress-slash-model Davy had been talking about marrying. Like Cher and Madonna, she only used one name.

"I guess you better come in," I said.

"Thanks." He scooped up his duffel bag and entered my apartment, looking around curiously. I didn't own much these days: a worn yellow sofa, a pair of white-and-yellow wingback chairs, a battered coffee table, and thanks to the miracle of Ikea, two tall wooden bookcases mostly devoted to bric-a-brac. No clocks, no calendar, no TV — nothing to remind me of the outside world. Nothing to stimulate my mind and set it racing again.

"How is Davy?" I asked.

"Good. He and Cree just left for Cancun."

"Oh? I thought he had business in New York tomorrow." At least, that's what he'd told me over the weekend.

Bob shrugged. "Cree's doing a photo shoot for *Sports Illustrated* — filling in at the last minute — so they decided to turn it into a vacation. They're flying out tonight. Probably already in the air."

He pulled off his coat, revealing an off-the-bargain-rack suit. I waved vaguely at the sofa.

"Sit down. Let me clean up. I wasn't expecting visitors. If you want a drink, help yourself — there's beer in the fridge."

* * * *

Twenty minutes later, I'd washed my face, run a razor over a three-day growth of beard, combed my hair, and put on nearly-clean slacks and a sweater. I almost felt human again, and I'd gotten rid of the worst of the whiskey smell.

Unfortunately, I had also begun to sober up, and with returning mental sharpness came all-too-familiar pains in both legs. Alcohol blunted my senses better than drugs; that's why I drank as much and as often as possible. I only stopped when I had to.

Finally I limped back out to the family room. Bob leaped up when he saw me, running one hand quickly across his nearly-shaved head and pulling his suit jacket straight.

"Let me guess," I said, really studying him for the first time. His too-short hair and well-developed muscles screamed military. "You just got out of the service and decided to pay his sister a visit. She suggested Davy might be able to find you a job."

He gaped. "Did you talk to Cree?"

Slowly I settled into one of the wingback chairs, folded my hands across my belly, and stretched out both legs; they hurt less that way.

I said: "Why else would an ex-Marine come to Philadelphia, if not to see your sister and her fiancé? You're dressed up — I assume

3

for a job interview — though I'd lose the baseball cap next time. But the *real* question," I said, warming to the subject, "is why Davy Hunt sent you here."

Bob frowned, brow furrowing. "He said he trusted your opinion. If you think I'm good enough, he'll take me on."

"In what capacity?"

"Bodyguard."

I raised my eyebrows slightly. "Davy needs a bodyguard?"

"My sister thinks so."

After their problem with blackmailers, I understood Cree's concern. Davy's net worth ran somewhere upwards of fifty million dollars — more than enough to make him a target for opportunists.

I opened my mouth, but before I could say anything, the doorbell rang again. From outside came faint childish giggles.

"You can start by taking care of those kids," I said to Bob. "Ask them not to bother me again."

"Sir!" Like a panther, he sprang to the door and threw it open. Ten-year-old boys scattered, screaming, as he gave chase. I heard Bob shouting something about "whupping hides" if they bothered me again, then several doors slammed shut.

When he returned, he was grinning. "I love kids," he said. "I don't think they'll bother you again, sir. At least, not for a few days."

"Thanks." Maybe bodyguards had their uses.

"Then you'll give me a try?"

I stared at him blankly. "I don't follow you."

"Sir, I'm supposed to be your bodyguard for the next few days. You can kick the tires. Try me out. Make sure I'm everything I ought to be to keep David safe."

"I don't *need* a bodyguard. I don't *want* a bodyguard. I leave my apartment once or twice a month at most!"

"David knew you'd say that." His brow furrowed. "He told me to tell you — beg your pardon, sir — to shut up and pitch in."

Just like Davy to be blunt with me. Maybe I *did* object too much. Maybe it *did* take a kick in the pants to get me moving. But did I really need a bodyguard?

It wasn't for me, though. It was for Davy. If he valued my opinion this much...well, I needed to get him a Christmas present anyway. This would be it, as I would let him know the next time I saw him!

"Very well." I motioned unhappily with one hand. I'd need rent money soon, anyway. "You can start bodyguarding in the morning. It's time I ran some errands, anyway."

Rent money meant a trip to Atlantic City and the casinos. Sometimes having a trick memory helped, like when I needed to know the number of face cards played from an eight-deck blackjack shoe.

"It'll be over sooner if I start tonight, sir."

"'Over sooner'?" I chuckled. "Bob, you sound like you don't want to babysit a seedy drunken cripple!"

"Sir!" He looked alarmed. "I never said that!"

"Then you *do* want to babysit a seedy drunken cripple?"

"That's a fool's argument, sir." He shrugged with wry humor. "You know I can't win. I just thought you'd want me out by Christmas day."

"I don't care. Start when you want. End when you want. It's all the same."

"Thank you, sir."

"Do you have a place to sleep?"

"Uh...not yet. I was hoping to bunk here."

It figured. Why did I suddenly feel like Oscar Madison from *The Odd Couple*, with an eager-beaver Felix about to move in?

"There's only one bed," I said, "and I'm usually passed out in it."

"The sofa is fine — after sleeping in a Humvee for six months, pretty much anything will do. Just give me a blanket and I'll be out like a log."

"There's one in the linen closet." I jerked my head toward the back of the apartment. "And an extra pillow on the top shelf."

Using my walking stick, I levered myself unsteadily to my feet. My legs ached again. Slowly I limped toward my bedroom, thoughts of Jack Daniel's and sweet oblivion dancing in my head.

* * * *

Sometime later — it could have been hours, it could have been days — a loud humming filled my ears. It took a few minutes, but I finally realized the noise came from outside my skull. It shrilled on and on, incessant and very annoying.

When I couldn't stand it any longer, I rolled over and opened my eyes. Daylight leaked in around the blinds, casting a pallid gray light over my bedroom. Groaning, I got my feet to the floor and sat up.

The world swung and tilted. My head throbbed and my eyes burned. It had been a long while since I'd felt this sick. Usually when pain and nausea and headaches hit, I can lie still and wait for them to pass. This humming grated on my nerves so much, though, that I rose and stumbled toward the door.

When I entered the kitchen, the noise grew louder. But what brought me up short was the brilliant, blinding light.

Every surface gleamed. Steel and chrome and glass shone and glistened. The burnt-out bulbs in the ceiling fixture had been replaced, the dishes in the sink had been washed, and my months-old collection of pizza boxes had disappeared from the counter. Underfoot, the white-with-gold-specks linoleum had a new glossy sheen. Even the trashcan had a fresh white plastic liner.

The humming came from the family room. Bob Charles slowly moved into view, pulling a little canister vacuum around the floor, sucking up dirt and dust bunnies. He wore a clean white shirt and tie, but had on the same brown pants as yesterday.

"Good morning," he called cheerfully, switching off the vacuum. "Ready for breakfast?"

"What do you think you're doing?" I demanded. My voice came out as a croak.

"Tidying up."

"Don't you know the difference between a maid and a bodyguard? I was still in bed!"

"It's ten-thirty in the morning. You've been asleep for more than sixteen hours, Pit. Half the day is gone!"

"Not asleep. Unconscious. Delightfully, *painlessly* unconscious. And how do you know my nickname?"

"Nickname?"

"Pit. Short for Pit-bull. Got it in college."

"Didn't you mention it yesterday?"

I shrugged. "Maybe."

But I hadn't. I could remember every word we had exchanged from the second I opened my front door to the second I'd gone to bed. Names, faces, facts, figures — I never forgot anything.

Maybe Davy had called me Pit, and Bob picked up on it subconsciously. I could only think of one other person besides Davy who still called me by my old nickname, and it seemed unlikely that Bob had ever met an organized crime figure like "Mr. Smith," as he called himself.

Bob was staring at my legs. I realized I hadn't put on a robe. Gray Jockey shorts didn't do much to hide the hideously scarred flesh running from my ankles to my hips.

Swallowing, Bob looked away. Pity — that was always the worst. It showed in his eyes.

"In case you're wondering," I said bitterly, "I got run over by a taxi." Everyone always wanted to know what had happened, even if they were too embarrassed to ask.

"David didn't say anything about that." Bob forced his gaze back to my face. "He did tell me to take you out for breakfast today, though — on him."

"I don't like going out. But maybe I'll make an exception this morning." Time to pay Davy back for sticking me with Cree's brother. I used to read *Gourmet* magazine; I knew some *very* expensive places to eat in Philadelphia.

* * * *

An hour later we left my apartment. Bob wanted to drive downtown in his battered old VW Rabbit, but I refused. Folding my legs into that tiny box of a car would have been torture.

Instead, we ambled up the sidewalk toward the Frankford El, our breaths pluming in the cold December air. The sun played hide-and-seek through holes in the clouds while an icy wind stirred leaves in the gutter. Far off, I heard an elevated train rumble past.

As we walked, Bob kept alert. Northwood is a small blue-collar section of Philadelphia, and it had definitely seen better years. But it was safe enough by daylight, and in the years I'd lived here, I had never had a problem beyond kids playing "bait the cripple" with my doorbell.

"This neighborhood is a dump," Bob said. "You should find a better place to live."

"I don't like change."

"Those kids over there —" He nodded toward a boarded-up rowhouse across the street where three teenagers in stocking caps watched us with predatory eyes. "They'd be happy to roll you for your cash."

"I think they're about to try it," I said. All three had gotten up and begun to cross the street toward us.

"Keep walking," Bob said. He turned to face the three. "I'll catch up in a minute."

"Do you need help?"

"I can take care of a couple of kids."

"Be careful." My mind started racing, taking in every detail. "The one on the left has a weapon in his pocket."

"How do you know?" Bob demanded.

"He keeps touching it through his pants. I don't think the others are armed."

"Get going."

"But —"

"Move!"

Spoken like a true bodyguard. I wasn't about to argue.

Turning, I limped quickly up the street. Motion caught my eye as I reached the corner. I half turned as a dark-skinned man in a gray silk suit seized my arm and propelled me toward the street.

"Relax, Mr. Geller," he said softly. "Mr. Smith wants to see you."

A white Lincoln Town Car roared up. Before it came to a stop, the back door popped open. My escort put his hand on the back of my head, pressing gently but firmly, and half guided, half pushed me into the lilac-scented back seat. Then he slid in next to me and slammed the door. We accelerated.

My abduction had taken less than five seconds. That had to be a record.

Twisting around, I gazed over my shoulder at the rapidly-receding figure of my bodyguard. Those three kids skirted my bodyguard and continued up the block. When Bob turned to check on me, a priceless look of shock appeared on his face. I had vanished. He began to run toward the Frankford El.

Turning back, I made myself comfortable, wincing a little as I uncrimped my legs.

"Hello, Pit," said a smooth voice beside me.

"Mr. Smith." I nodded to him. With his salt-and-pepper hair swept back and his neatly-manicured hands, he cut the perfect picture of a crime lord. As always, he wore an expensive Italian suit, blue this time with a white carnation at the lapel. "If you wanted to talk to me," I said, "a simple invitation would have sufficed."

"Not with your new, ah, *friend* looking on." Smith smiled a predator's smile. Since our paths first crossed, he had developed quite an interest in me — due no doubt to my trick memory, which had dredged up his real name from a chance meeting many years before. Since then, I knew he had been researching my life — even going so far as bugging my phone.

"What brings you to my neighborhood?" I asked.

"I would like you to meet my associate, Mr. Jones."

"Jones?" I raised my eyebrows and turned to the dark-skinned man next to me. "You've got to be kidding." Of African descent, with a diamond stud earring in his left ear, Mr. Jones seemed as fashionably well-groomed as Mr. Smith.

"Jones *is* my birth name," said Mr. Jones gravely. "Though I've been thinking of changing it to Tortelli to fit in better with the rest of the boys."

Mr. Smith gave a snort, then added, "Mr. Jones would not kid you about his name, Mr. Geller."

"Of course not." I sighed. Why did things like this always happen to me?

Then Smith lifted his left hand to my eye level. He held a miniature tape recorder. With his thumb, he pressed PLAY. Eleven beeps sounded — a phone being dialed. A moment later, I heard a woman answer:

"Hello?"

"Janice?" asked the voice of my bodyguard.

"Yeah."

"This is Bob. He went for it."

She laughed. "How fast can you get him to sign off on you?"

"A few days. God, he's depressing."

"Put a bullet in his head when you're done. Put him out of his misery. Can't have him talking to Hunt, anyway."

A chill went through me. Smith pressed the STOP button and returned the recorder to his pocket. It felt like I'd been struck in the stomach by a sledgehammer. Thank God I hadn't bothered to remove the bug in my telephone. Bob Charles had completely taken me in.

"Mr. Jones is in charge of your neighborhood," Smith said. "If you'd like your guest removed quietly, he will handle the extraction. As a personal favor to me, of course."

"Removed?" I said. "Extraction?"

"It is a specialty of mine." Mr. Jones smiled, showing beautiful white teeth.

"Uh...that won't be necessary," I said with a slight shudder. "I'd prefer to handle him myself."

Smith nodded. Mr. Jones passed me an ivory-colored business card with gold-embossed type. It said simply, JONES & ASSOCIATES and gave a phone number with a local exchange.

"If you need help, call me day or night," Jones said. "Any friend of Mr. Smith's is a friend of mine."

"Thank you." I pocketed his card. Not that I ever intended to call — but it would have been rude to refuse, and I thought it prudent to be very polite and very respectful to Mr. Jones.

Our Town Car glided to a stop in front of my apartment building. Mr. Jones got out, and awkwardly I did the same.

"Thank you," I said to Mr. Smith. "I owe you one."

"Yes, you do," he said.

Mr. Jones slipped back into the car, and they drove off together. I watched until they disappeared around the corner.

Suddenly, my life had gotten a lot more complicated.

* * * *

Bob returned to my apartment half an hour later, looking cold and annoyed. I let him in and deadbolted the door. Then I looked him over. Hard to believe he planned to kill me. I had always considered myself a pretty good judge of character, and he had fooled me completely. Damn it, I had actually begun to *like* him, with his goofy gung-ho act.

"No black eyes," I said, "and no bullet wounds, punctures, scuffs, or scrapes. Those boys must not have been much trouble after all."

"They knew enough to steer clear of me."

"See why I don't leave my apartment?" I limped back toward the kitchen. "It's an unpleasant world. And it's much too tiring."

"What happened to *you*?" Bob demanded, following. "I couldn't find you anywhere!"

"Oh, a friend gave me a lift home. I ordered a pizza. I hope you like pepperoni. It's the only topping that goes well with scotch."

I sagged into a well-padded kitchen chair and took a slice from the takeout box. Sal's Pizza & Hoagies had dropped it off five minutes ago. I had already poured myself a large drink — mostly soda-water, with just a splash of booze to give it the right smell, mostly for Bob's benefit. I couldn't appear to change my alcoholic behavior lest it tip him off that I knew too much.

"Pepperoni is fine." He got a beer from the fridge.

"Better stick with water," I told him, wagging a finger. "Bodyguards *never* drink on duty. Hazard of the trade."

Silently he put it back. I could tell it annoyed him, though. One point for me.

* * * *

After lunch, I announced my plans to visit the Free Library of Philadelphia...not our local branch, which specialized more in popular fiction than world-class research materials, but the large one on Vine Street in Center City. A plan had begun to form in the back of my mind...layers of deception, baited with promises of fast and easy money.

"The library? Can't you use the internet?" Bob asked. "Everything's online now."

"Not the material I'm looking for. And anyway, I'd still have to go to the library. I don't own a computer."

I didn't add that I blamed computers in part for the information-overload that had led to my nervous breakdown.

* * * *

On our second try, we reached the Frankford El without difficulty. I bought tokens; slowly we climbed up to the platform. Fortunately the train came quickly.

We sat in a nearly-empty car, and I focused my attention on the floor, analyzing stains and scuff-marks, trying not to look out the windows. Too much scenery, too much color and motion, tended to bring on anxiety attacks. I felt a rising sense of panic from Mr. Smith's warning. What would my fake-bodyguard do if I suddenly curled into a fetal ball on the floor?

"If we get separated," Bob said suddenly, "we need a plan. A place to regroup."

I looked at his face. "My apartment?"

"That will do if we're in this area. I meant someplace downtown, while we're out today."

"There's a House of Coffee at 20th and Vine. That's half a block from the library."

He nodded. "Good."

I went back to studying the floor. We rode in silence until we reached Race Street, and there we got out.

Shoppers bustled on the sidewalk, carrying bags and boxes, hurrying on holiday errands. Street vendors hawked caps and scarves and bric-a-brac. Brakes squealed and horns blared from the street. A bus rumbled past, spewing exhaust and carbon dioxide.

I felt a crawling sensation all over. Nervous jitters, just nervous jitters. Too many people and too much noise —

"Are you all right?" Bob asked.

I blinked rapidly, trying to stay focused. "I feel overwhelmed —"

"Come on." He grabbed my arm and propelled me forward. With his help, I managed to cross the street, and we headed toward Vine. I kept my gaze fixed on the sidewalk.

"Clear the way!" Bob bellowed. "Sick man coming through!"

To my surprise, people actually moved for him — shoppers, businessmen, kids, even a pair of nuns — and we made rapid progress. Finally we passed through the double doors and into the sanctuary of the Free Library. A soothing silence washed over me. Better, better, so much better here. I closed my eyes, just breathing, and felt muscles starting to uncoil.

Bob said softly, "If you need to go home —"

"I'll be fine. The outside world is...difficult sometimes. I shouldn't go into crowds on holidays." I swallowed. "I'm feeling better now. Really."

The card catalog of my youth had been replaced by computer terminals. I eased into a hard wooden chair, stretched my legs out as far as I could, and began my search for books on New York City banks.

Bob, with the occasional bored yawn, kept watch over my shoulder. I began jotting down titles and Dewey Decimal System numbers. When I had ten books selected, Bob took the list.

"I'll find them," he said.

Within twenty minutes, he returned with eight of the ten volumes. Not a bad average — he made a fair research assistant.

The Manhattan Federal Trust sounded like a good choice. After suffering a series of financial losses in the late 1960s, it merged with Third Continental Loan, forming the Manhattan Third Federal

Loan and Trust. It suffered a huge loss in 1973, when one of its armored cars had been hijacked. A half-dozen name-changes, mergers, and acquisitions later, I lost the trail in a 1991 Savings and Loan collapse. There didn't seem to be a surviving corporate entity.

I sat back. Yes, it would do nicely.

"Why do you care about this particular bank?" Bob asked suddenly.

"My father did some work there a long time ago," I said. "Can you find microfilm of back issues of the *New York Times*? I need to see July, 1973."

"The whole month?"

"Yes. And maybe part of August."

"You're the boss." Shrugging, he went to find a librarian.

Meanwhile, I returned to the computerized card catalog and began looking up volumes on the U.S. legal system — choosing more for titles than content. I had no intention of reading them if I could avoid it.

"You're in luck," Bob announced when he finally returned. "They have the *New York Times* going back over a hundred years on microfiche. A lady is setting up the viewer now. They have a private room you can use, too."

"Excellent!" I beamed as I handed over my new list. "When I'm done, I'll need these books. Can you find them?"

"Sure."

When he glanced at the titles, his eyes widened. Volumes like Circumventing the American Tax System, Overseas Tax Havens, and Criminal Statutes of Limitations: A State by State Guide must have caught him by surprise.

"What are you planning?" he asked.

"Bodyguards aren't supposed to ask questions," I said with a wink. "I'm doing some research."

"If this is illegal, I want to know. I might be held responsible as an accomplice —"

I laughed. "Since when is research a criminal act? I'm thinking of writing a book."

He frowned, clearly unsatisfied. But I offered no more explanations.

"Where do I go for the *Times*?" I asked.

"Over here." Turning, he led the way to a small room at the back of the library. An elderly woman had a machine set up for me, and while Bob went off to find my legal books, I began to skim newspaper headlines. Minutes ticked by. My bodyguard returned with a stack of hardbacks, then settled into the chair next to mine.

Finally, I found what I wanted: an article dated July 19, 1973. Five men made off with an estimated half million dollars in cash by hijacking an armored truck on the Brooklyn Bridge in broad daylight. It had been a daring robbery, ably executed.

"Way to go, Dad!" I muttered just loud enough for Bob to hear. Never mind that I hadn't been born yet when the robbery took place — thanks to my accident, I looked thirty years older than my actual age.

I printed out the article, folded it up, and stuck it in my shirt pocket. *Bait.* The library charged thirty cents for the printout, and I paid the lady happily.

"That's all I needed from the *Times*," I said as I limped out of the room. I found an empty reading table and pretended to study tax evasion and statutes of limitations for the next half hour. The volumes seemed interminable.

At last, just when I couldn't take it any more, my stomach growled, announcing dinnertime. Another chance to gouge my assassin-bodyguard? I'd see how far I could run up his credit cards before letting him off the hook.

"I don't think Davy would mind springing for dinner instead of breakfast," I told Bob, closing *Offshore Flight: Where and How to Take Your Money.*

"Probably not," he said.

"There's a little seafood house around the corner called Charley's Red. Supposed to be pretty good, too."

He perked up. "I could go for some surf and turf."

"You won't be disappointed."

How could he be? It was a four-star restaurant with a wine list to die for.

* * * *

Dinner was sublime. I ordered a bottle of Dom Perignon Rose 1988 with my caviar-and-truffle-stuffed lobster à la Charley. As I kept telling Bob throughout the meal, "Don't worry, it's on Davy."

Bob could only grin and nod. Finally, after a delightful chocolate soufflé followed by a glass of aged port, I could eat no more. I leaned back and patted my too-full belly.

Bob received the check and blanched. Dinner for the two of us came to almost $750, I saw. Not including tip.

"They expect a 25% gratuity," I told him, feeling generous: service *had* been exceptional.

"I... I'm afraid I can't, sir." He gulped. "There's only a couple hundred left on my credit card. David was going to reimburse me!"

"Oh." So much for running up Bob's credit cards. The possibility that my bodyguard might be broke had never occurred to me. "I'll handle it, then."

I pulled out my AmEx. At least I knew Bob's finances now. Could I somehow use that to my advantage? I would have to think on it.

After I signed the credit card receipt, I found I could barely stand. So much for keeping my head clear. I had no choice but to agree to a taxi — which Bob said he would pay for, to make up for dinner. We rode in warmth and comfort back to my apartment.

There, I set my trap. I accidentally "forgot" to remove the robbery article when I tossed my shirt into the bathroom hamper. I carefully left the lid up and the article in plain sight. Neat-freak that he was, I knew Bob would rush to close the hamper's lid, and when he did, he would spot the printout.

If he didn't conclude that my father had been in on the armored car heist, he was dumber than he looked. That, plus the research on offshore tax havens, painted me as a criminal at work...something he could try to turn to his advantage.

"Good night!" I said as I headed to my bedroom with a fresh bottle of whiskey. I carried it mostly for show; I had no intention of clouding my mind further tonight. "Oh, I'll be up early — we have to go to Atlantic City tomorrow."

"Want me to drive?" he offered.

"No need. Casinos return your bus fare in quarters when you get there, plus they sometimes throw in coupons for lunch and other freebies." I had a drawer full of Golden Nugget tee-shirts to prove it.

* * * *

As I lay in bed, thoughts racing, I mentally reviewed the recording Mr. Smith had played for me — and realized I had made a huge mistake.

Every button on a telephone keypad has a different sound. Since I remembered each tone on Mr. Smith's recording perfectly, it was a simple matter to match them up to numbers. Two seconds later, I had Joyce's phone number. If I'd thought of it in time, I could have used a reverse directory at the library to look up her name and address.

Calling myself a drunken idiot, I picked up my phone's receiver, punched number 4 so the dial tone went away, and said in a low voice: "Please tell Mr. Smith I'm going to the Azteca Casino on the nine o'clock bus tomorrow morning. When I get there, I'd like my bodyguard's complimentary drink spiked — something that will tie him up in the bathroom for an hour or so. I'm going to win a million dollars at the blackjack tables. Don't worry, I'll give it back. If Mr. Smith is willing to help, I'll owe him another favor. If not — well, I'll manage on my own."

I hung up. Then I opened my night table's drawer and removed four pens from the neat row inside, along with an unused pocket notebook. In tiny, cribbed lettering, I began making lists of fictional transactions using several different colors of ink and alternating between sloppy and neat handwriting. First came dates, then names of various casinos, and amounts I had won. At the bottom of each page, I noted the anonymous Swiss or Brazilian bank account into which the money had been wired. My fictional net worth climbed rapidly into the millions.

Of course, I included all the secret passcodes anyone might need to get the money out. I emphasized that part on the inside front cover: *Funds not accessible without account numbers and passcodes.* Bob would read those words first when he opened the notebook.

* * * *

My legs and back ached fiercely the next morning. When I couldn't take the pain any more, I rose and stumbled into the bathroom. I gulped four aspirins with a glass of tepid tap-water. God, I needed a real drink.

Someone had lowered the hamper's lid. I peeked inside. The printout in my shirt pocket had been removed, then put back — but not quite folded properly. Sloppy, sloppy work.

Returning to my room, chuckling to myself, I dressed in black Dockers and a navy blue shirt — more leftovers from my Wall Street days — then took a small suitcase from my closet and began to pack...underwear, socks, shirts, pants. Everything I'd need for an extended trip. I needed to convince Bob I planned on fleeing the country.

My bodyguard appeared in the doorway. "Going somewhere?"

"In case I decide to spend the night."

He nodded. "I'll bring my bag, too."

* * * *

An hour later we were on the bus. The drone of wheels on pavement, the murmur of little old ladies on their weekly gambling junket, the soft hiss of recycled air from the blowers overhead — I found it all curiously soothing. As I let myself relax, I began to open up and chat confidentially with Bob...part two of my plan.

"My father used to be involved with organized crime," I confessed in a low voice. Never mind that he had been a plumber. "He hijacked that armored car on the Brooklyn Bridge. The one I read about yesterday."

"What happened?" Bob asked. "Was he caught?"

"Not caught," I said. "Killed. His body turned up in the New Jersey wetlands near where Giants Stadium stands today. He had a bullet in his head, mob execution-style. I don't know what happened to the money, but I found out who did the hit a few years ago."

"Who?"

"Well...let's just say he's come a long way in the last thirty years. He runs the Azteca Casino. That's why I gamble there a lot — every dollar I take away is a little piece of my revenge."

He looked puzzled. "I thought odds favored the house."

"For most games." I chuckled. "You'd never guess I'm worth nearly as much as Davy Hunt, would you?"

He gaped at me. "Then why are you stuck in that shabby little apartment? You should live like a king!"

I lowered my voice confidentially. "Because," I said, "I don't want to attract the IRS's attention. If I started spending hundreds of thousands of dollars, they'd want to know where I got it."

"The tax havens," he said slowly. "That's why you were researching them!"

"Bingo."

He frowned. "Why are you telling *me*?"

"Because," I said grandly, "this is it. Today is my final day. I'm going to make one last big score and retire to Brazil while I wait for the statute of limitations on income tax evasion to pass. I want you to come with me as my bodyguard and assistant. I'll need help, and I think you're the man for the job."

He chewed his lip thoughtfully. This was a lot for him to consider. Would he go for it?

"If you're worried about salary," I added, "I'll pay you a lot better than Davy — starting with a $20,000 signing bonus as soon as our plane lands. That buys a lot in South America. When we come back, we'll both be set for life. What do you say?"

"It's a deal!" He offered his hand, and we shook on it.

Bait taken — hook, line, and sinker.

* * * *

Our bus rolled into Atlantic City on schedule and stopped at Bally's. We filed off with the old people, collecting vouchers for $20 in quarters, redeemable inside at the information booth. I shivered in the brisk wind while Bob collected our luggage. I should have worn a heavier coat.

"What next?" he asked, setting the bags down on the sideway.

"Go in and get our quarters, then we'll walk over to the Azteca."

He then ran inside with our vouchers. A few minutes later he came back carrying two rolls of quarters. Then, carrying our bags, we ambled toward the Azteca.

Shaped like a South American pyramid, the hotel-casino offered three hundred and thirty luxury hotel rooms, most with views of the Boardwalk and the Atlantic Ocean. The entire ground floor consisted of slot machines, gaming tables, bars, restaurants, shops, and two theaters for concerts and stage shows.

I surveyed the elbow-to-elbow holiday crowds. Too loud, too bright, too busy...your typical Atlantic City gambling hall. From experience, I knew I would need several stiff drinks to make it through the day. Adrenaline would keep me going for now, though.

"Where do we start?" Bob asked.

"Check our coats and bags," I said, "then take the quarters and play the slots slowly. Pretend you don't know me, but watch my back. Things will get crazy when I start winning big."

"How did you deal with it in the past?"

"I always kept my winnings under ten thousand per casino so they wouldn't catch on and blacklist me. Today, though, I'm going for broke. A million or more, all from the Azteca."

He whistled. "You can do that?"

"Trick brain, remember?" I tapped my forehead with an index finger. "Don't worry, I'll win. Just keep your eyes open and watch my back."

Without another word, I limped to the line of blackjack tables. I kept going until I found one where a cute Asian lady was shuffling fresh decks, and I took the chair farthest to the left. I'd see everyone

20

else's cards before mine. With 416 cards in play, knowing how many of each denomination remained in the shoe gave me a decided advantage, especially as we got toward the end.

I removed two hundred dollars from my billfold — gambling seed money, normally kept under my mattress — and bought a stack of chips. A man slid into the empty seat next to mine. I recognized Mr. Smith from the faint lilac scent.

"Good morning," I said without looking in his direction.

"That was quite a boast you made," he said. "A million dollars at blackjack?"

"I can do it, as you know."

He said, "That's why I'm here. I have to protect the casino's interests. You are a very dangerous man, Mr. Geller."

He set a tray of chips on the table before him — all bright pink and all stamped $100. He anted one. I risked $5. The three others at our table bet between $5 and $20.

The dealer began to draw cards from the shoe. A smattering of face cards and numbers for the others, a pair of jacks for Mr. Smith, a king and a four for me. Smith split his jacks, then hit for a twenty and a nineteen. I hit and drew an eight — busted. The house held at seventeen.

Nineteen cards gone. Four percent of the deck. A couple more hands and the odds would tilt in my favor.

Mr. Smith collected $200. The dealer swept away my $5 chip. We repeated. Mr. Smith won another $100, and I lost another $5. Repeat. I had a push, Smith lost. Repeat, and we both won.

A blonde in a skimpy mock-Aztec costume and too much eyeshadow approached. She had drinks on a tray.

"Compliments of the house," she said, setting them in the blackjack table's built-in cup holders. Ginger ale for Mr. Smith, watery scotch-and-soda for me.

"Thanks." I gulped mine in three swallows. "Bring me two more," I said before she disappeared.

Three more hands, sixty-seven cards burned. I increased my bet to $25. I split aces, then doubled down — easy wins. Three hands later, I increased my bets to $50. By that point, my initial investment had swelled to eight hundred dollars. Then twelve hundred. Then sixteen hundred.

Our dealer trashed the cards and began shuffling fresh decks together. My drinks arrived.

"You're good," said Mr. Smith, nodding.

"Yes," I agreed. I swallowed scotch-and-soda and felt myself relaxing, falling into the groove.

Suddenly Smith asked, "Would you like to play at a high-stakes table with the house's money? Management uses shills to keep the action hopping. There's nothing like a big spender on a winning streak to stir up the crowd."

"What about my bodyguard?"

"He's having that special drink you ordered right now."

Casually, I glanced over at the slots. Bob was chatting with a different waitress in a mock-Aztec outfit. She held out a little plastic glass of what looked like cola, and he took it. As he sipped, he casually glanced in my direction, but showed no sign of recognizing me. Good boy.

"Ten minutes," said Mr. Smith, "and you'll be on your own."

Ten minutes. Eight to ten hands.

"I can wait that long."

* * * *

It took almost fifteen minutes for Bob's drink to take effect. But when it hit, he hightailed it for the men's room at warp speed, leaving me alone.

I finished my hand — a $240 win — and tossed the dealer a $20 chip. Mr. Smith gathered up his winnings. By my count, I now had $7,600 in front of me.

"Follow me," Smith said.

He threaded his way through the blackjack and craps and roulette tables to a small door marked PRIVATE: EMPLOYEES ONLY. Inside, the noise and bustle of the casino gave way to fluorescent lights, cheap blue carpeting, and stark white walls broken only by glass doors showing tiny offices.

At the office marked CASINO MANAGER, Smith went in. I followed.

"Harvey," he said to the pudgy-faced man at the desk, "this is Mr. Geller, the guest I told you about."

"Hiya, Mr. Geller." Harvey wiped a sweaty hand on his pants before offering it to me. We shook. He went on, "I have your paperwork ready."

"Paperwork?" I asked.

"Legal forms you have to sign."

"Lawyers run everything now," said Mr. Smith half apologetically. "In the old days, Harvey would have broken your legs if you tried to skip with the casino's money. Now he'll have you arrested."

"What a kidder!" Harvey said, laughing. "Can you imagine *me* breaking anyone's legs?"

Actually, I couldn't. But since Mr. Smith seemed serious, I gave a shrug and a smile.

Harvey held out a clipboard. I skimmed the one-page form — I, Peter Geller, acknowledge that I am playing with the Azteca Casino Corporation's money, yada yada yada. I hereby warrant that all monies won or lost remain the sole and exclusive property of the Azteca Casino Corporation and will be surrendered before I leave the premises.

Harmless enough. I signed, pressing hard for three carbonless copies.

As soon as I finished, Harvey handed me the yellow copy from the bottom. Then he pushed a chip caddy loaded with gold chips stamped $1,000 across his desk. Ten stacks of ten chips each — one hundred thousand dollars. My hands began to tremble, and it wasn't from alcohol this time. I had never had this much money before...even if it wasn't mine to keep.

"What about my earlier winnings?" I asked.

"Give me your chips," said Harvey.

I did so. Harvey counted them quickly, took a lockbox from his drawer, opened it, and peeled seven crisp thousand-dollar bills and six hundreds from a roll. Without comment, he passed them to me.

"Thanks." I tucked them into my billfold.

"Come, Pit," said Mr. Smith with a smile. "A fortune awaits!"

* * * *

My bodyguard still hadn't returned. Uneasy and suddenly self-conscious, I settled down in the well-padded leather highboy seat at the left side of a high-stakes table in the center of the casino. Velvet ropes cordoned the players off from the general public, and floodlights bathed our seats in a warm yellow glow. Overhead, a blue neon sign blinked HIGH STAKES PLAYERS ONLY — $100,000 MINIMUM. I was the only player.

A young guy with his blond hair in a crewcut nodded to me, then began unsealing fresh packs of cards. As he shuffled, an elderly man with a string tie and cowboy hat settled into the highboy next to me. A girl brought him a tray with a quarter million dollars in chips. A few seconds later, an Arab — complete with robes and bodyguards — took the seat farthest right. I noted how the casino staff called him "your highness" and brought him drinks and bowls of green and red Christmas M&Ms without being asked. He had to be a regular.

I definitely felt out of my league.

Cowboy-hat seemed to sense my uneasiness. He jabbed me in the ribs with an elbow and said, "First time here in the spotlight, huh, son?" He had a slight drawl. I noticed the heavy silver ring on his left index finger said A & M — probably Texas A & M University.

"Yes, sir," I said.

"Internet money?" he asked.

"Mob money."

Cowboy-hat got real quiet after that. I shifted uneasily in my chair. Then Smith returned and patted me on the shoulder.

"Good luck," he said.

"Thanks. You're not playing?"

"I'll check back later. I have other duties."

"Of course."

Our dealer cleared his throat. "Ready, gentlemen?"

I threw out a $1,000 chip. Time to get the ball rolling.

If only it had been my money. Never had I seen such a lucky streak.

I won my first six opening hands as I began to count cards. I won most of the middle hands where I knew enough to guess what might turn up. I won all the late hands, where the odds had shifted in my favor. Weird, wacky, wonderful luck — where were you when I needed you, when that taxi ran me down?

My winning streak continued throughout the first hour. Shoe after shoe, I beat the house consistently. The dealer began paying me in $10,000 chips. I hadn't even known that denomination existed. My money grew...half a million, then nearly a million. Mr. Smith would never doubt me again.

And Smith had been right about the buzz a big winner created. Behind the velvet rope, a crowd gathered to cheer me on. I started to sweat; the whispers and bursts of applause pushed my senses toward overload. Those three watery scotch-and-sodas helped, but not nearly enough.

Suddenly I noticed Bob Charles at the front of the gawkers. He looked pale and shaky. He must have recovered from his sudden "stomach ailment."

"Mr. Smith says you need a drink," a voice said at my elbow. It was the same girl who had drugged Bob. She held out a tray. "Compliments of the house, sir."

"Thanks." Since everything in front of me belonged to the casino, I had no worries about being drugged.

It was another scotch-and-soda; I gulped it down. Strong this time, the way I liked.

"Bring me another?" I asked.

"Of course, sir." She vanished.

Tex leaned in close and said, "Better watch that stuff, if you expect to keep winning. Gotta stay sharp, son!"

"Drink or die," I said unhappily. "I can't function sober."

He laughed. "Then maybe I should take up drinking, the way my luck's running!"

His stack of chips had been cut in half over the last two hours. Further down the table, the prince barely held his own.

I bet $50,000 — and got a blackjack. Cowboy-hat drew to a 12 and busted. Too many face-cards still in play...with the dealer showing a five, I would have stayed.

My new drink came, and I downed it fast. The rising tide of voices began to grow muted; my hands stopped shaking. My world narrowed down to the cards.

But first, I reminded myself, I had to take care of Bob.

"I have to take a bathroom break," I said to the dealer. "May I leave my chips here?"

"Of course, sir."

"Don't worry, son," said Cowboy-hat. "I'll keep an eye on 'em for ya!"

"Thanks." I smiled wanly at him.

I rose, leaning heavily on my walking stick, and gave Bob a glance and a subtle follow-me jerk of my head. Then I limped to the men's room.

It was moderately busy inside. We stood side by side at the urinals, waiting until we were alone. Then I handed him my billfold with the $7,600 still inside.

"I have my million," I said. "There's a travel agency across the street. Buy two one-way tickets to Rio de Janeiro. I doubt if there's a direct flight from Atlantic City, but we should be able to make it with a couple of connections. Cut it as close as possible. When it's time to go, signal me. I'll cash out and we'll run for the plane. As fast as a cripple like me can run, anyway."

"Got it," he said.

* * * *

I returned to the high-stakes table and found Mr. Smith had replaced Cowboy-hat. My chips had not been touched. Fortunately for me, most of the watchers had dispersed.

Our dealer began shuffling new decks of cards.

"Is everything going as planned?" Smith asked.

"I think so."

"I saw your friend leave. You should have let Mr. Jones remove him for you, you know."

"Human life has value," I said.

"You should watch out for yourself, not someone who's trying to kill you."

I shrugged. "Perhaps I made a mistake. But I like him, and I think he's basically a decent guy. He just took a wrong step somewhere."

"Are you sure you won't change your mind?"

"I'm more stubborn than sensible. Besides, it's almost Christmas. 'Tis the season of brotherly love, and all that mushy holiday stuff. I couldn't have his 'removal' on my conscience."

"What's next?" Smith asked.

"Bob is out buying tickets to Rio de Janeiro. He'll be on the afternoon plane. That's where you come in."

"I suppose he needs a lift to the airport?"

"I'm going to cash out when he returns. I'll give instructions at the cashier's booth for the winnings to be wired into a nonexistent Brazilian bank account. Then, on my way out the door, someone can grab me, force me into a car, and drive off with me. Bob will think I'm being kidnapped and take off for Brazil alone."

"Why would he?"

"Because," I said smugly, "he's going to have my little black notebook with all the passcodes and bank account numbers. He'll think he's struck it rich."

"Until he gets there and finds out there's no money."

"Right."

"Then he'll come back, hunt you down, and kill you for making a fool out of him."

"He'll stay there. I'm sure he'll call once he gets to Rio and finds out he's been duped. I'll simply tell him he'll be arrested for conspiracy to commit murder if he returns to the United States. I imagine you still have that recording."

"Of course."

"I'll borrow it and play it back for him. He won't dare return. End of problem!"

Smith shook his head. "You overly complicate things, Pit. Remove him and move on with your life."

"That's not an option."

"Your plan is ridiculous."

"But you'll help me," I said.

He shrugged. "I find it fairly amusing. But once it's done, I have a real job for you in Las Vegas. One for which you are uniquely qualified."

"As long as I don't have to break the law," I said, "I'll go. I always keep my word."

The dealer asked, "Ready, gentlemen?" He had finished stacking the cards in the shoe.

Smith excused himself. The prince and I both anted, and our game began anew.

* * * *

By the time Bob returned, I had won another hundred and forty thousand. A new crowd gathered beyond the velvet ropes. Bob eased his way to the front and signaled me by tapping his wristwatch. Time to catch our plane.

"That's it for me," I said, rising. I tossed the dealer a $1,000 chip. "Thanks for everything."

"Thank *you*, sir!" he said, beaming.

I gathered my winnings onto a tray, then limped to the cashier's station. Mr. Smith sat comfortably ensconced behind the brass grill.

"How much did you win?" he asked in a low voice as I passed him my chips.

"One-point-two million," I whispered smugly, "plus change."

"It's a good thing you *were* playing with the house's money. How soon do you want to be abducted?"

"As we leave. We'll go through the doors onto Atlantic Avenue. Do you have a pen and paper?"

"Here." He slid them over to me.

I jotted down wiring instructions for the money and passed it back.

"Might as well go through the motions," I said. "May I have a receipt for the wire?"

Chuckling, he made one up. I tucked it into my little notebook, which I kept in hand as I limped off for the Atlantic Avenue doors. There Bob Charles waited impatiently, pretending to study a marquee. I paused beside him. From the corner of my eyes, I saw men in black suits starting to converge on us.

"I already wired the money to my Brazilian account from the courtesy counter. But I don't think they're going to let me leave here safely." Casually I dropped the notebook. "Cover that with your foot. Pick it up when I'm out the door — they can't find it on me. It has the passcodes for my anonymous bank accounts. If I can, I'll catch up at the airport."

Without bothering to retrieve my coat or bag from the checkroom, I headed for the door. The bellman opened it for me, and shivering at the sudden cold, I stepped outside.

Smith's men followed on my heels — goons built like refrigerators. I had seen both of them before at Smith's illegal casino outside of Philadelphia.

A white Town Car sat idling in front, and they grabbed my elbows and hustled me inside. I didn't struggle.

As I twisted around, we accelerated into traffic. I glimpsed Bob running out the front door. He stood there, staring after me, a look of anger on his face.

He cared what happened to me. I saw it, and in that moment I knew I had made the right decision. Better to handle him myself than let Smith and Jones do it. He *was* basically a decent guy.

"Thanks, fellows," I said to the goons.

Mr. Smith sat in the front passenger seat. He opened a small window in the bulletproof partition separating our seats.

"Where next?" he asked. "The airport?"

"Take a ten minute drive, then back to the casino. I have to pick up my coat and bag. Then I'll catch the bus home."

"You heard the man," Smith said to our chauffeur.

"Yes, sir!" he said.

The goons and I settled back.

* * * *

We didn't even make it five blocks — police cars with blinking lights cut us off, front and back. Our driver slammed on the brakes; we fishtailed, then came to a screeching halt.

As uniformed officers leaped from their cars with drawn weapons, Smith's goons reached for their guns.

"Don't do that," I said in a low voice. "This has to be a mistake."

A bullhorn blared: "Get out of the car with your hands up!"

"I'm not happy, Pit," said Mr. Smith. He got out of the car and raised his hands. The chauffeur and goons did the same.

Slowly, painfully, I followed.

"You are in big trouble," Smith told the policemen who advanced. "Do you know who I am?"

None replied. They forced his hands onto the roof of his Town Car and began frisking him. Another officer began reading us all our Miranda rights.

That's when I spotted Bob Charles sitting in one of the patrol cars. He must have gone running to the cops instead of taking off for Brazil with my money. I nodded to him, and he grinned back.

"That's him — that's Peter Geller!" he said, climbing out and pointing at me. "They were kidnapping him!"

A police lieutenant took my elbow and drew me to one side. "Mr. Charles flagged down a patrol car," he said, "and reported your abduction. He said you won big at the casino and they weren't going to let you keep it. Is that true?"

"No," I said emphatically. I gestured at the Town Car and Mr. Smith. "This is some kind of misunderstanding. I work for the casino. These men are all friends of mine. We were taking an early supper."

The lieutenant frowned. "What about the money he said you won? More than a million dollars, wasn't it?"

"Nonsense. I was playing with the casino's money. Here — see for yourself!"

I pulled out the yellow copy of the form I'd signed. The lieutenant scanned it, snorted, then said to the other cops:

"Let them go. We've made a mistake."

"Thank you," said Mr. Smith. He straightened his tie and jacket.

The lieutenant stalked back to Bob, and they exchanged heated words. Bob read the yellow form, then stared at me in disbelief. When the lieutenant made Bob get out and lean up against the hood of the police car, I watched with amusement.

Of course, the officer turned up two wallets — one of them mine — plus the notebook of bank account numbers and plane tickets. He studied them, then stalked back to me.

"Is this yours?" He held out my wallet.

"Yes. Bob was holding onto it for me."

He frowned. "And two tickets to Rio?"

"Also mine."

"Notebook?"

"Yep. Mine."

His eyes narrowed. He knew something odd had gone down, but for the life of him he couldn't figure it out.

"I think you all had better come with me to the station," he said.

I shrugged. "As you wish." To Mr. Smith, I said, "Perhaps you can recommend a good lawyer?"

"He'll meet us there," Smith said grumpily, reaching for his cell phone.

* * * *

I rode in the back of the police car with Bob. The cops hadn't bothered to handcuff either one of us. Mr. Smith and his goons were following in their Town Car.

"Are you insane?" Bob demanded. "I just saved your life! Why are you doing this to me?"

"Maybe I'm a little bit cranky, but I'm hardly insane." I chuckled. "You asked me to kick your tires, Bob. Congrats. You passed the test."

His breath caught in his throat. "A...test. This whole thing..."
"That's right. And I can *almost* recommend you to Davy Hunt."
"Almost?"
"There's one matter you still have to take care of."
He looked puzzled. "I don't understand..."
"Janice."
He paled. "How — how do you know —"
"Trick brain, remember?" I grinned. "Tell the police how Janice tried to set up Davy using the two of us, and I'll get you cleared of all charges by morning."

* * * *

Once Bob started talking to the police, he had quite a story to tell. When he got out of the Marines, an old girlfriend contacted him, got him to come to Philadelphia, and told him she worked as the private secretary for a billionaire sleazebag named David Chatham Hunt.

A year ago, Janice had a romantic fling with her boss. Presents were given, promises were made...apparently, she expected the relationship to go farther than Davy did. When he broke things off and started dating a supermodel named Cree, she took it very hard.

Janice planned her revenge with meticulous care. As his private secretary, she knew Davy's position on the board of directors at Hunt Industries was provisional. Any hint of a scandal, and he'd get the boot. Davy couldn't allow that to happen.

And that's where Bob came in. Janice knew about my friendship with Davy, and she thought my personal recommendation would get Bob hired as bodyguard, cutting through a lot of red tape. Apparently she believed she could lure Davy into a final romantic tryst...one where Bob would be present to take blackmail photos.

It could have worked. Davy might well have fallen into her trap. I could easily envision my old friend having one last fling with his secretary, just to get her off his back.

Once Janice was arrested, she collapsed into hysterics at the police station, confessed everything, and ultimately pleaded guilty to conspiracy charges. Her case would never go to trial, saving Davy a lot of embarrassment.

Thanks to Mr. Smith's lawyer, Bob Charles ended up with probation and stern warnings from a judge. He never spent a single night in jail. Best of all, on my recommendation, Davy hired him as his personal bodyguard. I thought they would go well together. Bob had certainly proved himself to my satisfaction.

* * * *

"And that's the whole story," I said to Davy and Cree over Christmas dinner. Cree had cooked it herself — a beautiful roast goose with cranberry sauce, mashed sweet potatoes, green bean casserole, and a delightful selection of home-baked pies.

"Incredible," Davy said, shaking his head. "You know what the worst part of this whole mess is?"

"What?" I asked.

"Janice was the best secretary I ever had."

Cree punched him on the arm — hard.

"But my new secretary seems just as good," he added quickly.

"Better," said Cree. She turned to me. "I picked him out myself. No more office romances, right, Davy?"

"Right!" he agreed. But he seemed a little wistful.

I chuckled. "It took a long time and cost a small fortune, but what do you think of *my* present?" I asked.

"Present?" Davy scratched his head and looked at Cree, who shrugged. "Did I miss something?"

I raised my wineglass in salute. "For the man who has everything — a new secretary and a new bodyguard. Merry Christmas, Davy!"

www.ingramcontent.com/pod-product-compliance
Lightning Source LLC
Chambersburg PA
CBHW050918120626
46552CB00004B/1646